Rabbit's Surprise Birthday

Julia Jarman
Illustrated by Charlotte Combe

Rabbit and Owl lived in a big, old oak tree. They loved their huge old tree. It made them feel safe and warm. They slept all day in the warm, cosy tree.

When night came Owl would wake up. He would open his eyes as wide as saucers. He loved to see the stars and moon twinkle in the night sky.

Every night Owl would fly down to see Rabbit. Every night Rabbit would wait for Owl. Then they would talk all night long. They had been very best friends for years.

One night Owl woke up and went to see Rabbit, but Rabbit wasn't there!

Owl called, "Hello, Rabbit." But Rabbit didn't answer.

Owl called again, "Rabbit! Rabbit! Where are you?"

Rabbit still didn't answer, so Owl went into Rabbit's burrow. Rabbit was there alone.

"Rabbit? Are you OK?" asked Owl. But Rabbit still didn't answer.

"Rabbit, my old friend, answer me," said Owl. But Rabbit didn't answer. He just looked down. Owl thought Rabbit looked very, very sad indeed.

So Owl hooted loudly.
He hooted like a fire engine.
He hooted like an ambulance.
He hooted like an owl who
wants his friend to smile.

Rabbit still didn't smile.
"What's the matter?" said Owl.
Rabbit still didn't answer.
"What's the matter, my old friend?" asked Owl.

"Owl, I am not **old**. I am eight," said Rabbit.

Owl didn't know what to say.

"I am eight," said Rabbit again. "I am eight **today**."

Then Owl **did** know what to say.

"Happy Birthday, Rabbit!" said Owl.

Rabbit still looked sad.
"Today is my birthday," he said, "but no one has remembered. No one has **ever** remembered. I have never had a **real** birthday."

Owl didn't know what to say, and he didn't know what to do. He needed to think but he could only think his best thoughts on his thinking branch at the top of the tree. So he flew up to his thinking branch.

Owl thought very hard.
"What is a **real** birthday?"
And then his best thoughts came.
He thought . . . birthday card.
He thought . . . birthday present.

And then his thoughts came faster and faster.
Birthday party!
Birthday games!
Birthday cake!

Then he had an even better thought. *Birthday cabbage!* Rabbit loved cabbage, and they could have the party in the garden with the big cabbage.

Owl flew to his hole as fast as he could. He wrote birthday invitations as fast as he could.

Then he gave out the invitations as fast as he could.

Then Owl flew down to the garden with the big cabbage. The stars lit up the cabbage patch.

"What a **lovely** place for a party," said Owl.

Then Owl flew to Rabbit's burrow.
"Rabbit!" he cried, "Come out!"
Rabbit came out. He looked startled.
"Follow me, quickly!" cried Owl.
So they raced off into the moonlit night.

Fox, Badger, Squirrel and Bat were in the garden.

"Happy Birthday!"

"Happy Birthday, Rabbit!"

"Eight today!"

They all had birthday presents for Rabbit. Bat even gave him a flying display! Bat flew upside down in the light of the moon.

"Wonderful!" thought Owl.

"Thank you! Thank you!" said Rabbit.
"What next?" he asked.
"Birthday party games?" asked Owl.
So they played Hopscotch and Pass the Carrot.

"Thank you! Thank you!" said Rabbit.
"What next?" he asked.
"Birthday cake?" asked Badger.
"Birthday **cabbage**!" said Owl.

Then Rabbit blew out the candle.
"You must make a birthday wish," said Owl.
"What could I wish for?" asked Rabbit. He gave lots of little jumps and one big one.
"You could wish for a slice of birthday cabbage," said Owl.

Later, Owl and Rabbit talked all night.
"Well, Rabbit," said Owl. "Was it a **real** birthday?"

"Oh yes," said Rabbit. "It was a **very** real birthday. Thank you so much, Owl."